DESMOND COLE
GHOST PATROL

THE SCARY LIBRARY SHUSHER

by **Andres Miedoso**
illustrated by **Victor Rivas**

LITTLE SIMON
New York   London   Toronto   Sydney   New Delhi

LITTLE SIMON
An imprint of
Simon & Schuster Children's Publishing Division
1230 Avenue of the Americas, New York, New York 10020
First Little Simon paperback edition September 2018
Copyright © 2018 by Simon & Schuster, Inc.
Also available in a Little Simon hardcover edition.
All rights reserved, including the right of reproduction
in whole or in part in any form.
LITTLE SIMON is a registered trademark of Simon & Schuster, Inc.,
and associated colophon is a trademark of Simon & Schuster, Inc.
For information about special discounts for bulk purchases, please contact
Simon & Schuster Special Sales at 1-866-506-1949 or
business@simonandschuster.com.
The Simon & Schuster Speakers Bureau can bring authors to your
live event. For more information or to book an event contact the
Simon & Schuster Speakers Bureau at 1-866-248-3049
or visit our website at www.simonspeakers.com.
Designed by Steve Scott
Manufactured in the United States of America 0719 MTN
2 4 6 8 10 9 7 5 3
This book has been cataloged with the Library of Congress.
ISBN 978-1-5344-2691-7 (paperback)
ISBN 978-1-5344-2692-4 (hardcover)
ISBN 978-1-5344-2693-1 (eBook)

CONTENTS

CHAPTER ONE

YOU CAN'T SCREAM IN A LIBRARY

Have you ever seen a library in a scary movie?

If you have, then you know they're usually old and dusty and very creepy. Floors creak. Book carts squeak. Libraries in scary movies look like they've been haunted *forever*!

But in real life, most libraries aren't like that at all. Actually, they're kind of cool. My family moves a lot, so I've seen a bunch of libraries in a bunch of places.

Some towns have old-fashioned libraries with stone steps and huge pillars. They have high ceilings and rows and rows of books. If you screamed your name inside a library like this, it would echo all the way around the room.

But remember, you can't scream in a library!

In other towns, the libraries are high-tech. They have computers everywhere, and touch screens and even automatic book machines. They're super fancy and super fun!

And some libraries are comfy and cozy. They have soft, slouchy chairs that make you want to sink right in with a good book and stay there for hours.

What's my favorite kind of library?
All of them, of course!
Why?
Because libraries are where the books are!

That's why I was excited to visit the Kersville Public Library for the first time since I'd moved to this town. I couldn't wait to see what kind of library it was going to be.

One thing was for sure: I *never* expected any of this!

That's me, Andres Miedoso, right there, behind all those thick, heavy cookbooks. The same ones that we built up like a fort in the middle of a book battle.

That's Desmond Cole. He's the only one brave enough or crazy enough to peek over the top of our book stack. Because if you saw what was on the other side, you would definitely scream.

And making noise in the library is what got us into this mess in the first place.

REMEMBER: NEVER DO THIS IN A LIBRARY.

You probably want to know how we ended up here, right? I kind of want to know too! Hmm, let me think. Well, I can tell you this: Our day didn't start out haunted. Not at all! It began like every other school day . . . with no ghosts in the class-room. Then we got a simple home-work assignment. Now I wonder if I'll ever do my homework again!

See, there's never a day without some kind of ghouly ghost trying to get your attention when you're part of the Ghost Patrol—even if you're at the library.

CHAPTER TWO

DR. ACKULA

It was a regular Monday morning, and Desmond and I were in class. Our teacher Dr. Ackula was telling us about our new assignment. If you ask me, Dr. Ackula kind of looked like a vampire.

But that's a different story.

Dr. Ackula was really nice, though if you ever meet him, never make the mistake of calling him *Mr.* Ackula. If you do, you will have to listen to him tell you about all about the years and years *and years* he spent in medical school. I made that mistake on my

first day at Kersville Elementary, and I haven't forgotten he's a doctor since.

The weird thing is that I still don't know why a doctor was teaching at our school!

But, like the vampire thing, that's a story for another time.

But I should get back to this story. Dr. Ackula told our class we were going to do research about our own town, Kersville. Everybody would need a partner, and luckily, Desmond and I were going to work together.

While Dr. Ackula walked around telling the others what they would research, I sat there getting worried. What if we got stuck researching the Kersville sewer system?

Just thinking about all that gross, stinky muck made me feel sick.

Desmond scooted his desk closer to mine. "Are you okay?"

I nodded. "I'm just worried about where we're going to have to go."

Desmond smiled. "I hope we get the new fire station. How cool would that be?"

I tried to think of what could go wrong there, but I couldn't think of anything bad.

They have cool uniforms and an even cooler truck. Not only that, but I'll bet they cook great food for all the firefighters too. Desmond was right. The fire station would be perfect. As long as we didn't actually have to put out any fires!

Turns out, I didn't have to worry about any of that. Desmond and I got a safe place for our assignment: the Kersville Public Library.

I let out a sigh of relief. No sewer, no fires. I turned to Desmond, expecting him to be disappointed, but he looked even happier than he would have been if we'd gotten the firehouse. His eyes were lit up, and his smile was big and broad.

Oh boy. I'd seen that look in his eyes before. Here's one thing I knew for sure: If Desmond Cole got this excited, it was time to run away! Fast!

Safe library or not, I had a bad feeling about this.

CHAPTER THREE

THE KERSVILLE PUBLIC LIBRARY

After school, Desmond and I went straight to the library. He still had that smile on his face and walked with a bounce in his step.

I hadn't been living in Kersville all that long, but I knew what made Desmond excited. *Ghosts.*

And everybody knew old books and ghosts went together like, well, school and homework.

My heart started to beat faster, but I started to walk slower. *Much slower.*

"What's wrong?" Desmond asked.

"I thought you wanted to go to the library."

"I do want to," I said, "but not if it's haunted." I swallowed hard.

"Haunted?" He looked at me like I was crazy. "Why would you think something like that?"

I wanted to say, *Because every scary movie ever has a haunted library in a haunted town. That's why!* But I didn't want Desmond to think I was scared for no reason.

So instead I asked him, "If it's not haunted, why are you so happy? I mean, libraries are cool, but they're not jump-up-and-down exciting."

Desmond laughed.

"Andres, you are wild. I don't love the library because it's haunted. I love it because where else can I find information on the really important things in life—aliens, monsters, and, of course, ghosts?" Desmond said.

"Um, the Internet?" I suggested. Desmond thought about this for a second. "Okay, yeah, that's true. But my mom won't let me stay online all night. However, she doesn't mind at all if I fall asleep reading a book."

That was true. My mom was the same way.

Desmond continued. "They have computers at the library too. So you get both books *and* the Internet. Plus, there are librarians to help if you have questions, no matter how weird. Did you know fleas can jump more than a hundred times the length of their own bodies? That would be like you jumping almost half a football field! Guess where I learned that?"

"At the library?" I asked, even though I knew that was the right answer. Then immediately, I started scratching my hair. Just thinking about fleas made me itchy all over.

Other than the itchies, I felt myself starting to calm down a little bit. Desmond was right. The library was full of books and computers and nice librarians. What was I so afraid of?

"Oh, c'mon!" Desmond said, and he started doing that bouncy-walk thing again.

So I followed behind him, trying to bounce too. I'm sure we looked really, really strange.

It didn't take long to get to the library, and when I saw it, I stopped bouncing . . . and started panicking.

That crazy library looked even more haunted than our haunted-looking school . . . and I didn't think that was possible.

It was an old building that was surrounded by dark trees with no leaves. There were a lot of windows that looked like eyes.

But what scared me the most were the statues. Even the creepy statues had creepy statues as pets!

Without knowing it, I started to walk backward, away from that strange library.

"Andres," Desmond said, "you're moving in the wrong direction."

I gulped, still staring up at the library.

Desmond grabbed my arm. "Dude, hurry up. We have work to do."

As Desmond dragged me inside, it looked like those window-eyes were watching us.

CHAPTER FOUR

MRS. SHOOSH

As soon as we stepped through the front doors, I was surprised to see that the library looked just like, well, like an old library. There were bookshelves everywhere and spiral staircases leading all the way to the upper sections.

And it was quiet.
So quiet you could
hear a flea sneeze!
I itched.

"This way," Desmond said, and we walked up to a woman sitting at the front desk. "Hi, Mrs. Shoosh. This is my friend Andres. He's new in town."

"Welcome to Kersville, Andres," she said. "I'm the librarian."

I smiled and said, "Thanks."

Mrs. Shoosh was not the kind of librarian I was expecting. She was sort of young for a grown-up. I thought a library like this would

have a gray-haired librarian who looked more like a fortune-teller with a crystal ball and wrinkly hands. Mrs. Shoosh wasn't like that at all. She looked cool.

Desmond told her about the report we were doing on the library, and she pointed us to the history section on the second floor. On the way, we passed the kids' section, so of course we had to stop.

I mean, they had one of the most amazing kids' sections I'd ever seen. And I've seen a ton of libraries! They had everything, including the newest issues of my favorite graphic novels and comic books.

Desmond headed straight for the scary books while I flipped through the latest Captain Awesome book. And for a few minutes we forgot what we were at the library to do.

That was when I got a feeling like someone was watching me. At first, I thought it was my imagination, just like when I thought the library had eyes. Then I looked down the row of books into the grown-up section. I saw an older woman staring in my direction.

Something about her gave me a bad feeling, but I wanted to finish reading my book.

So I tried to ignore her. But I could still feel her staring at me.

When I looked over again, she wasn't so far away anymore. She had moved closer to us.

I dropped the book onto the table and ran over to Desmond. He was holding a huge book about monsters.

"D-Desmond," I whispered to him. "There's a woman over there, and I think she's watching us." I pulled him over to where I was standing, so he could see the strange woman for himself, but she wasn't there.

The mystery woman was gone.

CHAPTER FIVE

HITTING THE BOOKS

"I'm telling you," I whispered to Desmond. "There was a woman, and she was staring right at me. It was freaky!"

"Then where did she go?" Desmond asked.

I shrugged. "I don't know."

It *was* pretty strange how she had disappeared so quickly. Where could she have gone so fast?

Desmond patted me on the back. "Maybe it was your imagination," he said. "You know how you get."

I stared at him for a few seconds with my mouth hanging open. "Wow! You don't believe me?" I asked. "I'm telling you that she was here!"

Desmond shrugged. "Maybe she wanted the book you were reading."

"Captain Awesome?" I asked. "Really?"

"You never know," Desmond said, laughing. "Look, forget about it. We have to get to the history section and work on our report."

I'd almost forgotten all about that.

Desmond went over and returned the monster book to the shelf, but as we walked away, we heard the book fall to the floor. The loud thud echoed around the quiet library.

Then Desmond walked back and replaced the book, but it fell again. The sound was even louder this time.

That's when we heard a craggy woman's voice say *"Shhhhhhhhh."*

It was the longest, creepiest sound I'd ever heard. So creepy that it gave me the *shhhhhhhhhhh*ivers!

SHHHHHHHHHHHH!

To make matters even weirder, there was nobody around. . . . I mean, *nobody*! Desmond and I were totally alone in the kids' section. Remember the shivers I talked about? They ran from my toes up to my hair.

Desmond picked up the book and put it back on the shelf for the third time.

And it fell off for the third time.

But Desmond was ready this time. He caught the book before it could hit the ground. "Did you see that catch?" he asked me, holding the book up in the air, like he had just made the play of the game in the World Series.

Just then all the other books on the shelf started to shake. My eyes opened wide. My lips moved, but I couldn't speak, especially because what happened next was unbelievable.

One by one, the books floated off the shelf *all by themselves*!

Then they started flapping their covers like wings until, suddenly, the flying books swooped down toward Desmond.

My best friend was under attack!

"Arrrrrrghhhhh," Desmond called out, trying to shield himself.

Desmond was completely shocked. And so was I. But I couldn't just stand there. I had to rescue him.

Without thinking about it, I ran over to him and started batting away the books. I had heard of "hitting

the books," but this was ridiculous!

As we battled, Desmond and I looked at each other, and we knew what we had to do. It was Ghost Patrol time!

But first we needed to warn Mrs. Shoosh.

CHAPTER SIX

MESS. NO MESS.

"Right this way," Desmond said a few minutes later. We brought the librarian, Mrs. Shoosh, back to the scene of the weirdness. "I'm sorry to have to show you this, but take a look!" Desmond exclaimed, pointing to the mess.

The mess that wasn't there!

The kids' section had been totally wrecked, but now it was back to normal. All the books that had been flying around the room were placed neatly back on the shelf in order.

"What happened?" Desmond asked.

"That's impossible," I said.

Mrs. Shoosh looked from Desmond to me. "Boys, I think you've been reading too many scary stories," she said.

"I don't even like scary stories," I mumbled, but Mrs. Shoosh didn't hear me. She was too busy walking away, leaving us alone again.

That's when Desmond leaned in and whispered to me, "Don't worry about Mrs. Shoosh. You and I know what we saw, right?"

I nodded. "I will never ever look at a book the same way again."

"This is serious," Desmond said. "You know what we have to do, right?"

I gulped. *"We?"* I asked nervously.

"We have to save the library." That same excitement I saw earlier was back in Desmond's eyes. "Let's start in the ghost story section. The *grown-up* ghost story section."

ADULT SECTION

Desmond grabbed my arm and pulled me up a spiral staircase, which was old and rickety. Every step we took made a creaky squeal. We were near the top when we heard another *"Shhhhhhhhhh."*

Again, there was nobody around. Desmond and I ran down the hall. My heart was beating at double speed. When we got to the section with ghost stories, there were plenty of scary books.

Luckily, there were *no* ghosts!

I picked up a book called *Ghost Stories for Scaredy-Cats*, which was kind of a silly title. But after a few pages, I slammed the book back onto the shelf. It was way too scary for a scaredy-cat like me.

That was when I heard someone scream. And it was loud!

Desmond ran toward the scream. That's one thing I don't understand. I mean, why would anyone run *toward* danger? But Desmond was a run-into-danger kind of kid.

I followed him, even though I really didn't want to know where that scream had come from. All we saw was a woman hugging a book, but it wasn't the woman who had been spying on me earlier.

Desmond yelled, "The book is attacking her!" He ran over to the woman and tried to wrestle the book away from her.

But the woman was not going to let that book go. "What is wrong with you?" she asked Desmond. "I've been waiting to read this book for three months! How dare you try to take it away from me?"

Desmond stepped away from her and apologized. "Sorry. I thought . . . um . . . Sorry."

The woman looked at the book and screamed again. I guess she was really excited about that book.

That's when we heard another *"Shhhhhhhhhh."*

The woman shot us a look like she thought we had said it, but the shushing noise came from the next room over.

As the woman walked away with her prized book, Desmond grabbed my arm. Before I could stop him, he pushed me into the computer lab. This time we weren't running toward a scream. We were running toward a shush.

COMPUTER
LAB

75

CHAPTER SEVEN

SHHHHHHHHHH

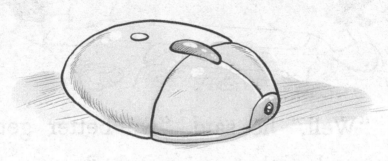

The lab was completely empty, but all the computers were turned on. If anyone had been here and said "Shhhhhhhhhh," then they were gone now.

Desmond sighed like he was upset there weren't any ghosts around.

"Well," he said, "we better get started on that assignment."

"Finally," I told him. Doing our homework probably wouldn't be as much fun as reading, but at least I wouldn't be scared.

We sat at the computers and started looking up information about the library.

"Check this out," Desmond said. I looked over and saw a photo from a newspaper. In the black-and-white picture, a man was cutting a ribbon on the new library building in front of a crowd of people.

KERSVILLE PUBLIC LIBRARY
GRAND OPENING

"Wow, that's an old picture," I said, noticing that it was faded. One woman in the crowd looked almost see-through. "Let's print it out and use it in our report."

Desmond went to save the picture when all the computers in the room turned off. Then the whole room went completely dark.

A chill ran through my body. It felt like the temperature in the room dropped, and goose bumps sprung up on the back of my neck.

Desmond shivered too. "Interesting" was all he said.

"Do you mean 'interesting' like you turned everything off from your computer?" I asked.

"No," Desmond said. "'Interesting' like I don't think we're alone."

I did not want to hear that.

Suddenly, all the computers turned back on. In the darkness, we could hear typing, and whoever was typing was doing it really fast. Like really, really, *really* fast.

Plus, they were typing the same

thing on every single computer. *At the same time.*

It was just one very long word: Shhhhhhhhhh.

Something really ghosty was going on, and I didn't want to stick around to figure it out.

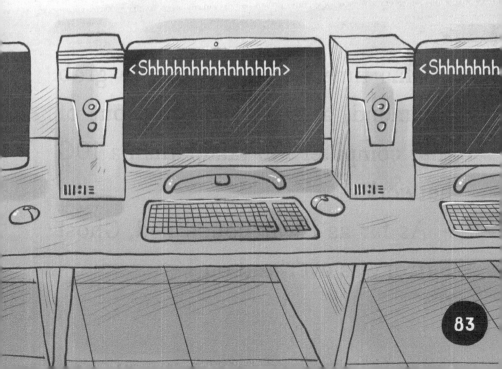

This time I was the one to grab Desmond, and I pulled him out of that computer lab faster than a 10G network.

As far as I was concerned, Ghost Patrol was over and out!

We hadn't even gone ten feet when
we bumped into someone.

Someone as thin as a piece of cardboard.

Well, actually, it *was* a piece of cardboard. It was a life-size cutout of some grown-up dude wearing a hat and a fancy suit. I slammed on the brakes, and Desmond tripped over me and landed on the floor.

"Are you both okay?" Mrs. Shoosh asked us. She didn't even say anything about us running in the library.

Desmond had a huge smile on his face. He pointed to the cutout. "Whoa, that's the famous scary story author Damon Chilling. He's my favorite writer!"

"Then you should stick around," Mrs. Shoosh said. "He's going to be stopping by in an hour to read from his new kids' book."

As another person waved for Mrs. Shoosh's help, Desmond turned to me. "C'mon, Andres. It's up to us to stop that ghost. We can't let it ruin Damon Chilling's reading!"

CHAPTER EIGHT

GHOST TRAPS

Desmond and I headed for the map room next. I wasn't sure what he was up to, but when Desmond Cole is hunting ghosts, nothing will stop him.

Desmond searched through a bunch of maps until he found the one he was looking for.

He took it out and unrolled it. It was a map of the library.

"Here," Desmond said, pointing to the kids' section. "This is where Damon Chilling is going to read today."

"But what can you do to stop the ghost?" I asked.

Desmond pointed to another room on the second level. "The question is, what can *we* do to stop the ghost. And the answer is simple. We set up a ghost trap. Right here."

"Um, did you say *ghost trap*?" I could feel fluttering inside my stomach.

Ever since I'd moved to Kersville, I had seen my share of ghosts, and they never seemed easy to trap. They seemed to be able to get out of anything!

"Trust me," Desmond said. "I know ghosts."

I nodded. He was right. He did know a whole lot about ghosts. A lot more than I did, that was for sure. But what was a *ghost trap*?

Desmond rolled up the map and put it back on the shelf. "Listen. Ghosts haunt places because they want something. They don't do it just for fun."

"Makes sense," I said.

"If a ghost haunts a doughnut shop, it's probably because he likes doughnuts," Desmond said.

*If I were a ghost,
I would haunt the
arcade. That would
be awesome!*

"I bet this ghost loves books," Desmond continued. "So, let's give her some books!"

We ran to the area that Desmond had pointed out on the map. "We are going to build a book fort," Desmond said. "That will be the perfect ghost trap!"

A half hour later, Desmond and I had built a book fort to end all book forts. It was amazing! We must have used every book from at least four shelves.

Mrs. Shoosh seemed to be really cool, but I was seriously worried about what she'd say when she saw this. It would take her forever to put all these books back where they belonged.

"Don't worry, Andres," Desmond said. "We'll fix everything when we're done." Sometimes it felt like he could read my mind.

"Cool," I said, and started to feel a little better.

That is until the ghost showed up.

CHAPTER NINE

CHILLING?

Here's the thing about ghost traps. Sometimes things go wrong.

And this was one of those times!

On one hand, Desmond was right. The ghost *did* show up. She floated right into the room and headed straight for the book fort.

Desmond and I hid, waiting for her to see all those books and start reading.

But on the other hand, Desmond was wrong. He thought the library ghost must be interested in books, but she wasn't. She floated right past them.

And headed straight for us!

That's how Desmond and I ended up in our current situation.

As the ghost got closer and closer, I shook and shook in my hiding place behind those huge cookbooks.

But Desmond was trying to be a superhero. "Tell us what you want!" he demanded as the ghost hovered over us.

I covered my eyes, but through my fingers I could see the ghost's green face. With her glasses perched low on her nose, she pointed directly at Desmond and let out a loud *"SHHHHHHHHHHHHHHHHHHH!"*

It was so loud and so strong, wind whipped up and started blowing. It blew so hard, I thought it was going to blow the hair right off my head!

The good thing was that her shush was so powerful, it blew most of the books right back onto the shelves.

The bad thing was that without the books, Desmond and I had no fortress and no ghost trap. So we backed up against a wall as the ghost loomed over us.

Finally, she whispered in a raspy voice, "What time is Chilling?"

"Chilling?" Was that some kind of scary ghost term? What did it mean?

"Do you mean the Damon Chilling reading?" Desmond asked her. "His reading starts in a little while."

"Oh, I can't wait," the ghost said, and she actually smiled. "I'm a big fan of his work!"

"Me too!" Desmond agreed.

I couldn't believe it. Desmond Cole just made friends with another ghost! The ghost sighed.

"I've had trouble reading books lately. The words are so blurry! So now I have to listen to people read if I want to enjoy books." She pointed to both of us. "But I can't hear them read with loud people like you in the library."

Desmond thought for a minute while I just stood there trying to stop my teeth from chattering.

Suddenly, he picked up a book from the table and held it out. "Can you hold this for me?"

The ghost reached out to take the book, but her ghost hand missed it by a mile.

"Hmm," Desmond said. "Just like I thought."

That was when Desmond got that look in his eyes. I knew what that meant.

Desmond had an idea.

CHAPTER TEN

GREEN, LOUD ETHEL

It turns out, the Scary Library Shusher is actually named Ethel, and she's kind of nice, once you get over the green color . . . and all that loud shushing.

It was Desmond who figured out Ethel's problem. Her glasses were old. Like really, really old!

They were so old that they didn't help her see anymore. She was having a hard time reading.

So we called Zax, the ghost who lives in my basement. He could fix anything. I should know. That ghost has fixed just about everything in my house . . . even if it wasn't broken!

Zax came to the library to fix Ethel's glasses. She was so happy that she gave him a tight hug, one ghost to another. "Now I can see every word," she exclaimed. "And I won't have to shush anyone again. I felt so rude doing that."

In the lost and found, Desmond found a hat and a jacket for Ethel to wear. And we got her to the Damon Chilling reading just in time. His book had tons of chills and thrills.

When he was done, Ethel cheered the loudest, and I think she surprised everyone there—even Chilling!

To thank us for our help, Ethel stuck around to give Desmond and me a hand with our report. That ghost knew everything about the library. In fact, she told us she was there when the library first opened.

Desmond and I looked at each other, completely surprised.

"Wait a minute," Desmond said, and found the newspaper photo we had saved on the computer.

"That's *you*!" I said, pointing to the part of the picture I thought was faded. Now that I looked closely, it was the outline of a woman. A ghost.

It was Ethel!

"It was an exciting day," Ethel said, and she laughed. "Even way back then, I loved books. And thanks to you two and Zax, I can read again!"

"Tell us more about the library, Ethel," Desmond said, getting ready to take notes.

"Yeah, tell us everything," I added, smiling.

It had been a wild day, but with Ethel's help, we were going to totally ace our report.

I guess it's true what they say. . . .

It helps to have friendly
ghosts in haunted places!